To Mary Kathryn 4/07

Islands in Heaven

by Pamela Santi Meunier
Illustrated by Susanne Egan

Islands in Heaven

Written by Pamela Santi Meunier
Illustrated by Susanne Egan

For inquires contact Santi Meunier @
Galactica Press 25 Hamilton Ave. Jamestown, RI 02835-1274
Galactca@aol.com, 1-800-335-8553 (US only)
(401) 423-3330.

To contact Susanne Egan:
susanneegansart@hotmail.com

Also available at Galactica Press:

ANGELS WITH FUR, Inspirational Stories For Animal Lovers
THE OBSIDIAN TRIALS, Seven Spiritual Steps for Overcoming Our Fears

Galactica Press
800-335-8553 galactca@aol.com

First Edition

Printed in Hong Kong

IBSN 0-9669095-2-6

Toby Drewe-Williams was an individual. She had fiery red hair, eyes as blue as the sea, and a smile that made even the grumpiest people laugh. Toby encouraged everyone to be themselves and follow their dreams. Everyone loved Toby, and she loved everyone.

Toby lived on an idyllic island off the rocky coast of Maine with her parents, her sister Elisabeth, and her dog Rascal. Her favorite time of year was summer, when the air was filled with the smell of pine trees, honeysuckle, and salty sea breezes. Purple lupine flowers, as tall as Toby, covered the grassy hills that led down to the water's edge.

Toby cared about everything on earth, and spoke to the rocks, flowers, and people as if they were all the same. Everyone and everything had value and deserved her time and attention. Everywhere she went she cast a brilliant light.

Each morning during summer vacation Toby and her dog Rascal would set off on an adventure. Toby never went anywhere without her bucket, because she never knew what treasures she might find.

Everywhere she looked there were starfish, seashells, garden snails, wood for carving, or a fossil rock, just waiting to be found.

At eight o'clock every morning, Toby and Rascal would wave to the ferry as it came in from the mainland, and then run over to see if there were any chores needing to be done at Green's Market. Toby loved to unpack boxes and use the pricing gun.

Mrs. Green always rewarded Toby for her hard work with a double scoop ice cream cone with chocolate sprinkles all over it. Rascal licked up all the drippings.

Every evening Toby and Rascal would return home with lots of treasures and adventures to share. Each night when she said her prayers she would thank God for her wonderful family and for her beautiful island.

Summer came to an end much too soon. Toby and Rascal watched the ferry filled with tourists leaving for another year. It was quiet once again as the islanders prepared for a long peaceful winter.

Every day Rascal would wait for Toby outside the school gate. Toby's sister Elisabeth was very pretty and always had lots of boys willing to walk her home. Rascal was Toby's best friend.

On this particular day, Rascal waited and waited, but Toby didn't come out of school. The doctor went rushing in and then Rascal saw Toby's parents go in. Rascal was very worried. Toby was so sick she had to be taken to the big hospital on the mainland.

Rascal stayed with Mrs. Green at the store and waited, and waited. A dark cloud slowly covered the island as everyone waited to hear the news about Toby.

Toby was in a deep, deep sleep. No matter what the doctor did, Toby did not stir. Her family gathered around and prayed for her to be all right. They prayed and prayed, but Toby still did not move. Sometimes, no matter how hard we pray for something, God has other plans.

Off in the distance, Toby's slumber was broken by a sweet voice asking her to awaken. Her body felt very heavy, but her spirit was as light as a feather so she opened her inner eyes. When she did, she saw a magnificent angel standing before her.

He was so beautiful. His presence filled her with peace and happiness.

"I have come to take you to Heaven, Toby. God has seen your brilliant light and is very pleased with you."

Toby was torn between excitement and concern, “I'm not sure. I don't want to leave my family and my wonderful island. It is the most beautiful place in the world. Are there islands in Heaven?”

The angel answered her, “Yes, there are islands in Heaven, and God has a very special one just for you and your family. They will join you there when it is their time. Until then you will have everything you want in Heaven.”

Toby gleefully jumped into the arms of her angel, blowing love and kisses to her family as they flew off.

But her family could not see or feel her joy. All they felt was a deep aching sadness in their hearts.

Months and months passed and the dark cloud over the island remained. Toby's family, her friends, and her sweet island were not the same without her.

It was as if all the joy had left the island when she died. Toby watched from heaven as the dark cloud grew thicker and thicker. Her heart welled up with sadness and she began to sob. Immediately, her angel appeared to see what was wrong. It is very unusual to hear crying in Heaven.

Toby said to her angel, “You said I would have everything I wanted here, but the thing I want most I do not have at all.”

Puzzled, the angel asked, “What is it that causes you so much sadness?”

Toby replied, "How can I be happy in Heaven, when everyone I love on earth is so sad? I have to go back and let them know that I'm all right so they can be happy again, too. Please help me. It is all that I truly want."

God overheard Toby's wish and granted her permission to go to earth for just one more day. God told Toby that she would have to use all her love and imagination to communicate, because no one would be able to see or hear her.

Toby jumped for joy. "Thank you, God! I know I'll find a way."

Toby then climbed into the arms of her beloved angel and off they flew towards earth. As they approached the island, the sky grew darker and darker. Once on the deck of her house she could see the cloud's shadow on the water.

Toby knew she had to act quickly, but what could she do? She had to find the answer for herself. She had learned that angels never give us an answer that we need to find within ourselves. Toby remembered God's words: "You must find the solution in your love and imagination."

Toby spotted her favorite bucket sitting empty on the deck. The tide was coming in and Toby couldn't resist lowering the bucket to see what gifts the sea would place inside. Soon her bucket was overflowing with treasures. Each wave brought in a special treat: a starfish, beach glass, and even an old sneaker.

Suddenly, she heard Rascal running and barking as he approached her. He stopped in his tracks. He cocked his head from side to side and Toby laughed.

"You can see me! Come here, Boy." Rascal ran into Toby's arms, wagging his tail and licking her face. "I don't know how you can see me, but I sure am glad you can, dear friend. Maybe you can help me. I have to let everyone know that I am happy and all right, so this horrible cloud will leave."

Rascal barked his approval.

Toby grabbed her bucket of treasures and began to make her rounds with Rascal, as they always had in the past. First, they saw the ferry off and then they walked over to Green's Market. Toby walked in and began to look nostalgically around when suddenly she noticed her sandy feet left footprints on the wood floor. At first she was afraid that Mrs. Green would get mad, but then she had a wonderful idea.

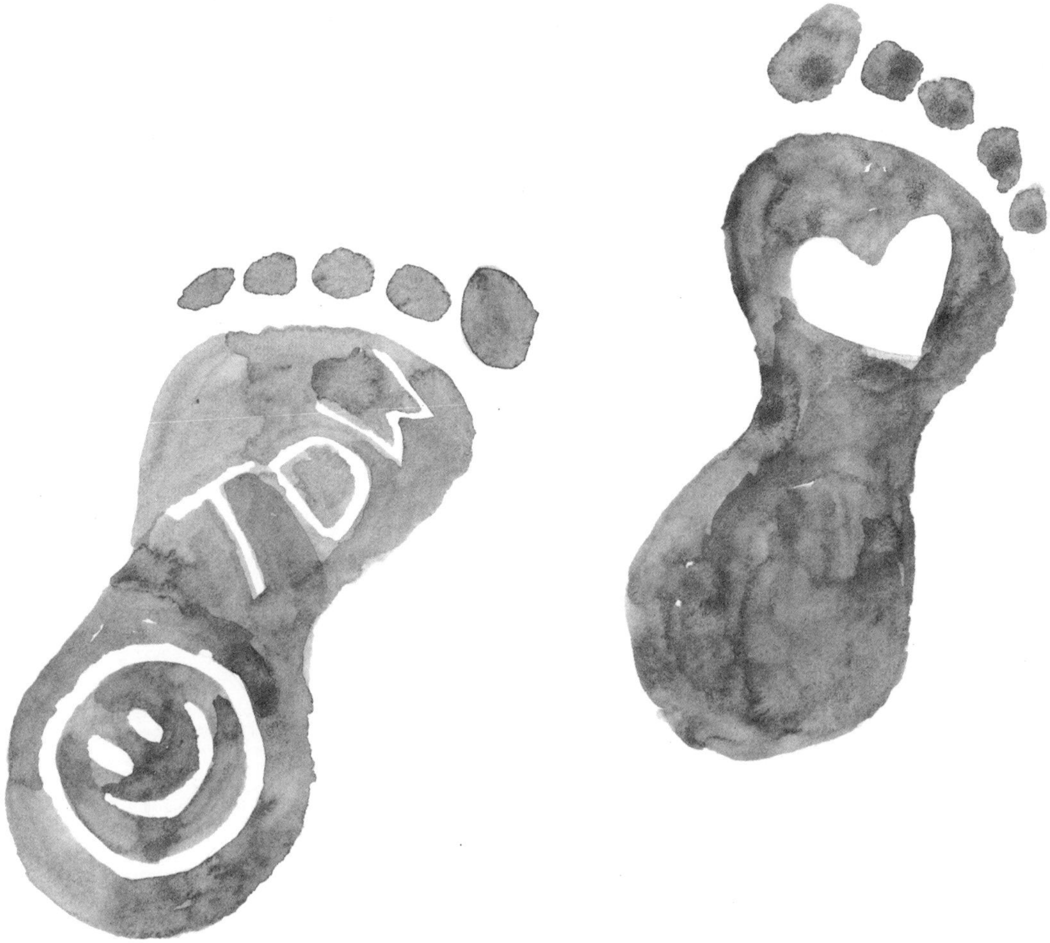

She made a heart in one footprint and a smiley face in the other with her initials T.D.W.

"This is it!" Toby exclaimed. "This will be my way of showing everyone I love that I am safe."

Excitedly, she and Rascal hurried off to the school to her sister's cubby and left her mark next to Elisabeth's coat and hat. She left her footprints all over the island, along with something special from her bucket. Home was her last stop.

She left her sign in the kitchen with a beautiful piece of beach glass, in the tub with a starfish, and finally on the dock with the bucket and the old sneaker. Excitedly, she waited for her family to come home.

Mom came into the house first, her arms filled with groceries. She did not notice Toby's sign. Toby tried to get her attention, but could not. Mom was so surrounded by sadness she could not see anything else.

"Angel, help me. Help my Mom to see my sign." Toby's eyes began to tear up.

Her angel comforted her. "You have done well. They will see. Just be patient."

Elisabeth ran into the house, crying with joy. "Mom! Mom! Toby was at school. She left her footprints and her initials in my cubby along with this shell!"

Mom shook her head, "How can you play such a dirty trick on me. Toby is dead. She is gone!"

Toby's mom sat down at the table and cried, knocking some of the groceries onto the floor. As she reached down to pick them up she spotted Toby's footprints and gasped. "Elisabeth, look here! Is this what you saw at school?"

Elisabeth hugged her mother and nodded as she picked up the perfect piece of blue beach glass. It was the color of Toby's eyes.

"It's a sign! My little girl is all right, she is all right!" her mother cried, with tears of joy and relief.

Toby looked out the window as everyone came rushing down the walk, carrying Toby's treasures. All of her friends were laughing and crying joyfully. How wonderful it was to see them. How Toby wished she could hug them. Once again, the kitchen was filled with happiness.

Toby spotted her father coming home, slowly walking out to the end of the dock. His head hung low, as if he were carrying a great weight on his shoulders. He did not know why everyone was gathered in the kitchen. He just knew that he wanted no part of fun and laughter since he lost his little girl.

Toby and her angel followed him onto the dock.

He leaned on the rail, watching the sunset. The cloud over the island was almost gone. No one had seen a sunset since Toby's death. It was a bright red sunset, the color of Toby's hair.

Her father noticed the bucket with the old sneaker; the rope from the bucket was still wet. He looked confused and then spotted her footprints. In amazement, he knelt down to touch them.

Mom saw him from the kitchen window. She ran to him to explain. Again, tears filled their eyes as Toby's memory comforted their heavy hearts. The last cloud lifted as her dad held Toby's bucket in his arms.

Everyone ran outside. They laughed and cried and hugged each other while Rascal barked happily and wagged his tail.

As the last trace of gray left the sky, Toby's angel said, “It's time to go.”

“This is all I wanted. Thank you Angel, and thank you, God, for letting me come.”

"Good-bye, Rascal. Take care of them for me. I'll be waiting for you all."

Toby then climbed into her angel's arms and flew back to her island in Heaven.

This book is dedicated in loving memory to

Jessie Daniell Bullens-Crewe

My beloved God-Child

&

A Brilliant Light

Special Acknowledgement

To my best friend, Cindy Bullens-Crewe, her husband Dan, and their daughter Reid- Jessie's family. I want to extend my gratitude to all of you for your friendship, love, and quiet strength. It has been both a comfort and an inspiration.

I have written this story for you and families like yours who have lost precious children. It is a tribute to their loving memory, and I hope, a comfort to those of us who have been left behind.

Until we are all reunited, may God bless you.

A special note of gratitude to A.N. whose generosity helped make this book possible.